Howdy Reveille!

Aimee Aryal

Illustrated by Megan Craig

MASCOT BOOKS

www.mascotbooks.com

It was a beautiful fall day at
Texas A&M University.

Reveille was on her way to Kyle Field
to watch a football game.
Let's follow her around Aggieland.

She ran across Simpson Drill Field
and passed the Corps of Cadets as
they practiced marching.

The cadets shouted,
"Howdy Reveille!"

Reveille stopped at the Century Tree.

A couple sitting on a bench said,
"Howdy Reveille!"

Reveille walked to the
Academic Building.

A professor passing by waved,
"Howdy Reveille!"

Reveille went over to the
Memorial Student Center.

Some students standing nearby yelled,
"Howdy Reveille!"

It was almost time for the football game.
As Reveille walked to the stadium,
she passed by some former students.

FIELD

The former students remembered Reveille
from when they went to Texas A&M.
They said, "Howdy, again, Reveille!"

Finally, Reveille arrived at Kyle Field.

As she ran onto the football field,
the 12th Man cheered,
"Gig 'em Aggies!"

Reveille watched the game from
the sidelines and barked for the team.

The Aggies scored six points!
The quarterback shouted,
"Touchdown Reveille!"

At half-time the Fightin' Texas Aggie Band
performed on the field.

Reveille and the crowd listened to the
"The Spirit of Aggieland."

The Texas A&M Aggies
won the football game!

Reveille ran up to Coach Franchione.
The coach gave her a pat and said,
"Great game Reveille!"

After the football game,
Reveille was tired. It had been
a long day at Texas A&M.

She walked home and climbed into bed.

"Goodnight Reveille."

For Anna and Maya, and all of
Reveille's little fans. ~ AA

Dedicated to Matt, Mishu, and Axle for being such a caring
and supportive family to me. ~ MC

Special thanks to:

Scott Elles

Dennis Franchione

Mike McKenzie

Rosa Rodriguez

For information please contact Mascot Books,
P.O. Box 220157, Chantilly, VA 20153-0157.

TEXAS AGGIES, TEXAS A&M UNIVERSITY, TEXAS A&M, FIGHTIN' TEXAS AGGIE BAND, AGGIES,
GIG 'EM AGGIES, TEXAS AGGIE BONFIRE, THE TWELFTH MAN and 12th MAN are trademarks
or registered trademarks of Texas A&M University and are used under license.

ISBN: 1-932888-18-7

Printed in the United States.

www.mascotbooks.com